SHARON BOOGIES

HAAGEN DA'SPOTLIGHT

KAYE FANTÁSTICA

AMINA TWIRLARINA

SLEEPING JUDY

If You're a DRAG QUEEN and You Know It

by

Lil Miss Hot Mess

Illustrated by

Olga de Dios

RP | KIDS
PHILADELPHIA

To Michelle, Juli, and Virgie, for your visionary leadership.
And to Zev, Vega, Cal, and the next generation of queens-in-training.
—L.M.H.M.

For the Queer Youth.
—O.D.D.

Running Press Kids
Hachette Book Group
1290 Avenue of the Americas, New York, NY 10104
www.runningpress.com/rpkids
@RP_Kids

Printed in China

First Edition: May 2022

Published by Running Press Kids, an imprint of Perseus Books, LLC, a subsidiary of Hachette Book Group, Inc. The Running Press Kids name and logo is a trademark of the Hachette Book Group.

The Hachette Speakers Bureau provides a wide range of authors for speaking events. To find out more, go to www.hachettespeakersbureau.com or call (866) 376-6591.

The publisher is not responsible for websites (or their content) that are not owned by the publisher.

Print book cover and interior design by Frances J. Soo Ping Chow.

Library of Congress Cataloging-in-Publication Data
Names: Lil Miss Hot Mess, author. | Dios, Olga de, 1979- illustrator.
Title: If you're a drag queen and you know it / by Lil Miss Hot Mess; illustrated by Olga de Dios.
Other titles: If you are a drag queen and you know it Description: First edition. |
New York, NY: Running Press Kids, 2022. | Audience: Ages 4-8.
Identifiers: LCCN 2021002917 (print) | LCCN 2021002918 (ebook) | ISBN 9780762475339 (hardcover) | ISBN 9780762475315 (ebook) | ISBN 9780762475322 (ebook) | ISBN 9780762475346 (ebook) | ISBN 9780762478378 (ebook) Subjects: LCSH: Children's songs, English—United States—Texts. | CYAC: Drag queens—Songs and music. | Happiness—Songs and music. | Songs. | Singing games. Classification: LCC PZ8.3.L556 If 2022 (print) | LCC PZ8.3.L556 (ebook) | DDC 782.42 [E]—dc23 LC record available at https://lccn.loc.gov/2021002917 LC ebook record available at https://lccn.loc.gov/2021002918

ISBNs: 978-0-7624-7533-9 (hardcover), 978-0-7624-7837-8 (ebook), 978-0-7624-7532-2 (ebook), 978-0-7624-7534-6 (ebook)

APS

10 9 8 7 6 5 4 3 2 1

If you're a drag queen and you know it . . .

BLOW A KISS!

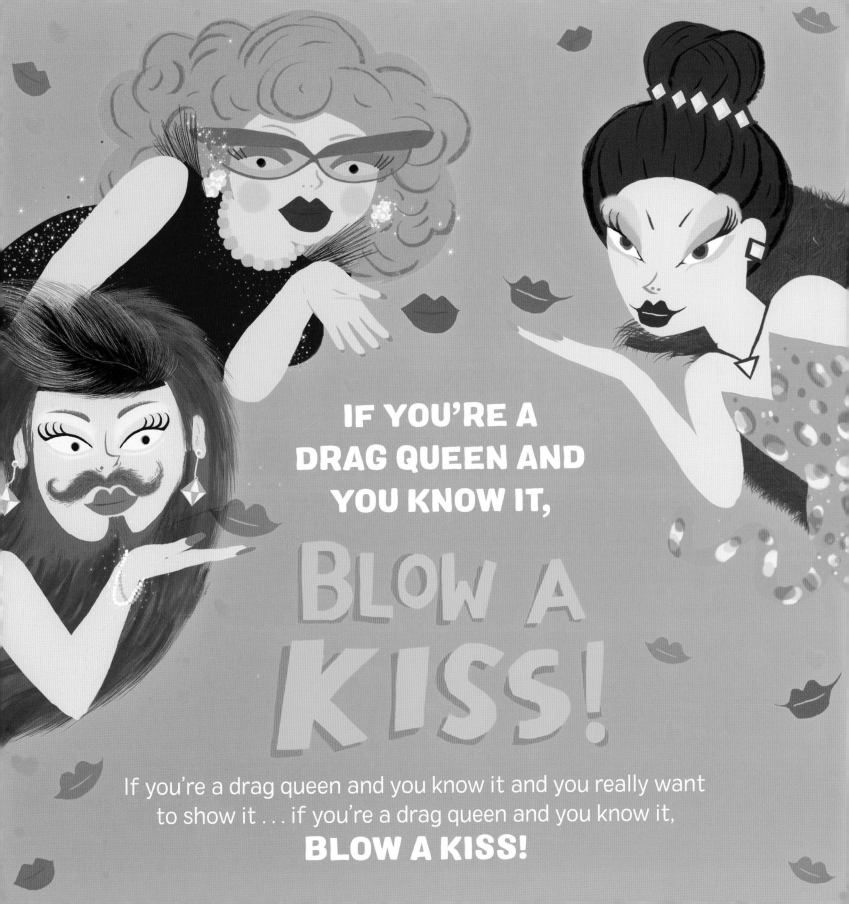

IF YOU'RE A DRAG QUEEN AND YOU KNOW IT,

BLOW A KISS!

If you're a drag queen and you know it and you really want to show it . . . if you're a drag queen and you know it, **BLOW A KISS!**

If you're a drag queen and you know it . . .

STRIKE A POSE!

IF YOU'RE A
DRAG QUEEN AND
YOU KNOW IT,

STRIKE A POSE!

If you're a drag queen and you know it and you really want
to show it . . . if you're a drag queen and you know it,
STRIKE A POSE!

If you're a drag queen and you know it . . .
SAY "TAA-DAAA!"

IF YOU'RE A DRAG QUEEN AND YOU KNOW IT,

SAY "TAA-DAAA!"

If you're a drag queen and you know it and you really want to show it . . . if you're a drag queen and you know it, **SAY "TAA-DAAA!"**

BLOW A KISS!

STRIKE A POSE!

If you're a drag queen and you know it . . .

DO ALL THREE!

SAY "TAA-DAAA!"

If you're a drag queen and you know it,
DO ALL THREE.

If you're a drag queen and you know it and you really want to show it . . . if you're a drag queen and you know it, do all three!

GIVE A WINK!

IF YOU'RE A DRAG QUEEN AND YOU KNOW IT,

GIVE A WINK!

If you're a drag queen and you know it and you really want to show it . . . if you're a drag queen and you know it, **GIVE A WINK!**

If you're a drag queen and you know it . . .
SHAKE YOUR BUM!

IF YOU'RE A DRAG QUEEN AND YOU KNOW IT,

SHAKE YOUR BUM!

If you're a drag queen and you know it
and you really want to show it . . .
if you're a drag queen and you know it,
SHAKE YOUR BUM!

If you're a drag queen and you know it . . .
LAUGH REAL BIG!

IF YOU'RE A DRAG QUEEN AND YOU KNOW IT,

LAUGH REAL BIG!

If you're a drag queen and you know it
and you really want to show it . . .
if you're a drag queen and you know it,
LAUGH REAL BIG!

GIVE A WINK!

SHAKE YOUR BUM!

If you're a drag queen and you know it . . .

DO ALL THREE!

LAUGH REAL BIG!

If you're a drag queen and you know it,
DO ALL THREE.

If you're a drag queen and you know it and you really want to show it . . . if you're a drag queen and you know it, do all three!

MOUTH THE WORDS!

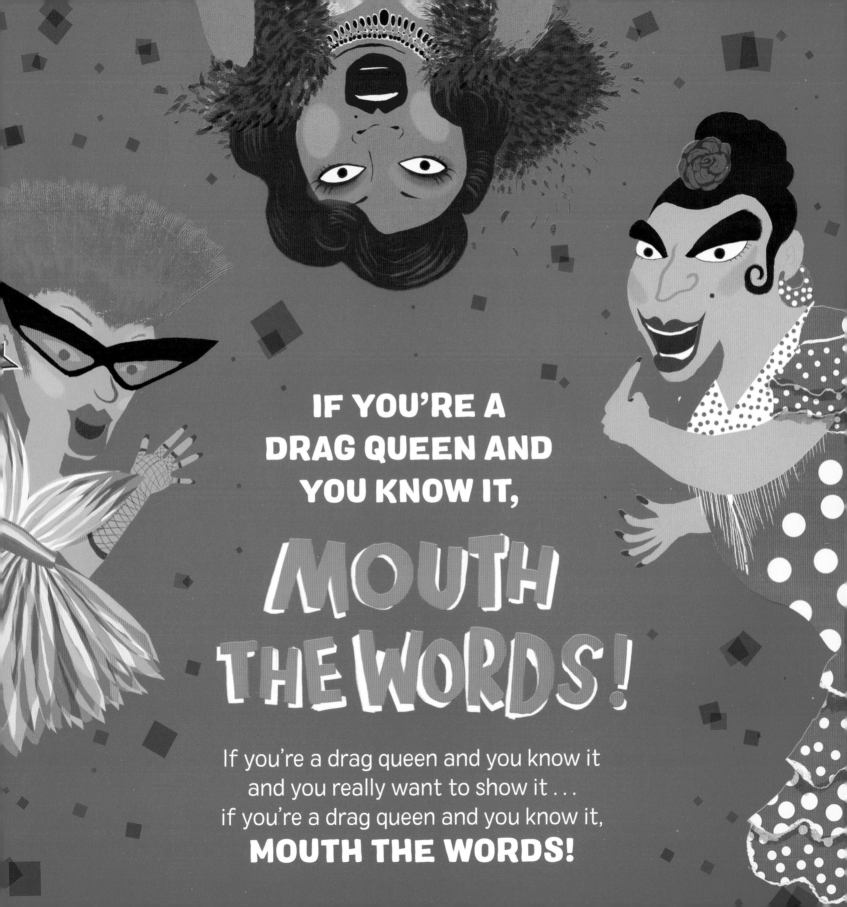

**IF YOU'RE A
DRAG QUEEN AND
YOU KNOW IT,**

MOUTH
THE WORDS!

If you're a drag queen and you know it
and you really want to show it . . .
if you're a drag queen and you know it,
MOUTH THE WORDS!

If you're a drag queen and you know it . . .

TWIRL AROUND!

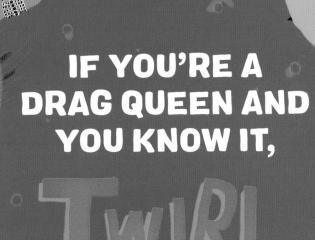

**IF YOU'RE A
DRAG QUEEN AND
YOU KNOW IT,**

TWIRL
AROUND!

If you're a drag queen and you know it
and you really want to show it . . .
if you're a drag queen and you know it,
TWIRL AROUND!

If you're a drag queen and you know it . . .
SHOUT "YESSS QUEEN!"

IF YOU'RE A DRAG QUEEN AND YOU KNOW IT, SHOUT "YESSS QUEEN!"

If you're a drag queen and you know it and you really want to show it . . . if you're a drag queen and you know it, **SHOUT "YESSS QUEEN!"**

MOUTH THE WORDS!

TWIRL AROUND!

If you're a drag queen and you know it . . .

DO ALL THREE!

If you're a drag queen and you know it and you really want to show it . . . if you're a drag queen and you know it,

DO ALL THREE!

RETTA BOOKE

KITTY CABOODLE

SÍ REINA DEL MAR

MINI QUEENIE MINEY MO